On Christmas Morning

by Jane Belk Moncure
illustrated by
Kathryn Hutton

Published by The Dandelion House
A Division of The Child's World

for distribution by VICTOR
BOOKS a division of SP Publications, Inc.
WHEATON, ILLINOIS 60187

Offices also in
Whitby, Ontario, Canada
Amersham-on-the-Hill, Bucks, England

To the teacher or parent:

On Christmas Morning contains a unique approach to the birth of Jesus. It will delight young children as they imagine themselves present on the night Jesus was born.

Children are constantly dramatizing events. Through imaginative play, a child learns and comes to better understand characters, situations, and events.

This book will open up the possibilities of such creative drama. Hearing the "story," the young child will readily pretend to be an angel singing, a shepherd running, a bell ringing, a lamb leaping, the wind blowing, etc.

Use the book to provide a framework for children to express—through creative dramatics—their feelings about the birth of Jesus.

Published by The Dandelion House, A Division of The Child's World, Inc.
© 1983 SP Publications, Inc. All rights reserved. Printed in U.S.A.

A Book for Preschoolers.

Library of Congress Cataloging in Publication Data

Moncure, Jane Belk.
  On Christmas morning.

  Summary: A child imagines what he would do for Jesus on Christmas morning if he were the wind, a lamb, a wise man, Joseph, Mary, etc. Includes the words and music for "Christmas is a Happy Time."
    1. Christmas—Juvenile literature.   [1. Christmas]
  I. Hutton, Kathryn, ill.   II. Title.
  BV45.M583   1983   394.2'68282   83-10104
  ISBN 0-89693-210-9

1 2 3 4 5 6 7 8 9 10 11 12 R 90 89 88 87 86 85 84 83

On Christmas Morning

What is Christmas?
It's a special time
when I can praise God
that Jesus was born.

If I were an angel
    on Christmas morning,
I would sing loudly
    to the shepherds—
sing about baby Jesus
    in the manger.
That's what I would do.

If I were a shepherd
 on Christmas morning,
I would run—
 run fast to the stable
 to see. . .

little Lord Jesus
in the manger.
That's what I would do.

If I were a church bell
   on Christmas morning,
I would swing up and down
   and ring my bell.
   "Ding-dong. Ding-dong.
   Christ is born.
   Christ is born."
That's what I would do.

If I were a lamb
on Christmas morning,
I would leap through the
meadow, singing,
"Baa, baa, baby Jesus.
I'm so glad you are born!"

If I were a donkey
    on Christmas morning,
I would gallop
    to the stable, braying,
"I'm glad,
    baby Jesus.
I'm so glad you are born."

If I were the wind
    on Christmas morning,
I would blow softly
    over baby Jesus
    in the manger—
    whispering,
"I'm so glad you are born."

If I were Joseph
on Christmas morning,
I would open wide the door
to the stable. . .

open the door
    and let everyone in
        to see the baby Jesus.

If I were Mary
    on Christmas morning,
I would hold Jesus
    in my arms. . .
    and rock. . .
    and sing him
    a lullaby song!
That's what I would do!

If I were a camel
    on Christmas morning,
I would walk
    with very big steps.
Walk toward Bethlehem.
    Walk! Walk!
Walking to find
    the little Lord Jesus.

If I were a star
on Christmas morning,
I would shine
even in the day!

I would shine like
   bright morning sunshine,
twinkling,
   "Happy Christmas Day!"

If I were a Wise man
   on Christmas morning,
I would hurry to find
   the little Lord Jesus.
Hurry to find
   God's own Son.

But because I am me,

I will clap my hands.

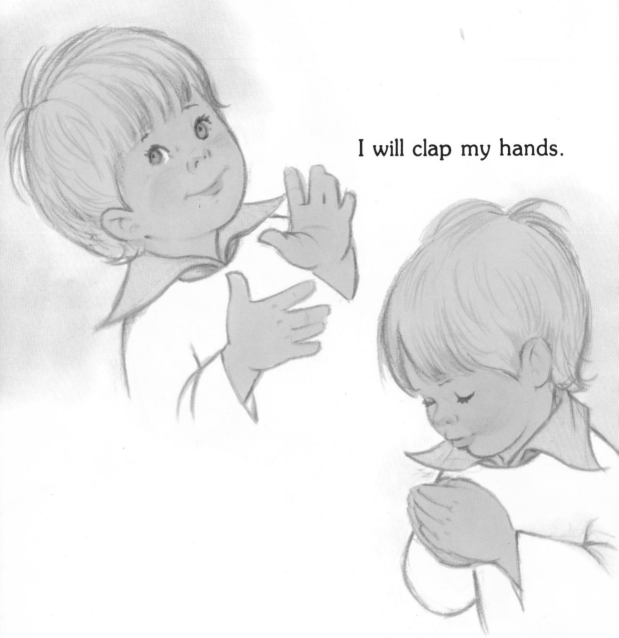

I will say, "Thank You for baby Jesus."

I will bring an offering.

I will sing because
Jesus is born.

I will sing because
   Jesus loves me.
That is why He came
   long ago!
I will sing because
   it is Christmas—
   Jesus' birthday!

Christmas Is A Happy Time

DOROTHY BRAUN

ELLEN THOMPSON

Ding, dong, ding, dong. Christ-mas is a hap-py time; I will tell you why.

Christ-mas is a hap-py time; I will tell you why. God sent Je - sus

to be born, On that first glad Christ-mas morn. Christ-mas is a hap-py time.

That's the rea - son why. (Also suitable for Youth Choir and/or Handbell Choir.)